The Greatest Shepherd of All

A REALLY WOOLLY Christmas Story

Illustrated by Julie Sawyer Phillips

Written by Holley Gerth

Scripture taken from the International Children's Bible®

www.dayspring.com

www.tommynelson.com

A Division of Thomas Nelson, Inc.

www.ThomasNelson.com

The Greatest Shepherd of All

Book design by Koechel Peterson & Associates, Inc., Minneapolis, Minnesota

Library of Congress Cataloging-in-Publication Data

Gerth, Holley.
The greatest shepherd of all : a really woolly Christmas story /
illustrated by Julie Sawyer Phillips ; written by Holley Gerth.
p. cm.
Summary: On Christmas Eve, Grandpa Woolly shares with three excited
youngsters the story of the birth of Baby Jesus, and how three young
sheep, much like themselves, met this greatest of all shepherds.
ISBN 13: 978-1-4003-0964-1
ISBN 10: 1-4003-0964-6
[1. Sheep—Fiction. 2. Shepherds—Fiction. 3. Jesus
Christ—Nativity—Fiction.] I. Phillips, Julie Sawyer, ill. II. Title.
PZ7.G3252Gre 2006
[E]—dc22

2006012258

Printed in China

1 2 3 4 5 / MT / 10 09 07 08 06

I am the Good Shepherd;
I know My sheep...
and My sheep know Me.
JOHN 10:14 ICB

t was Christmas Eve and Grandpa Woolly
was just settling down
in his corner of the pasture.

Suddenly, he heard the rustle of little hooves
in the grass. He looked up to see
three lambs quickly scurry behind a bush.

He shook his head and smiled,
"Faith, Hope, Joy, I know you're out there."

Three little heads sheepishly
poked out from behind the bush.

Sawyer

"What are you doing up? It's way past your bedtime,"
said Grandpa Woolly.

"We're too excited to sleep!"
Joy exclaimed.

"We can't wait for Christmas to come," said Hope.

"And, most of all, we wanted to hear the story," said Faith.

"What story?" asked Grandpa Woolly,
pretending not to know what they were talking about.

"You know the one! The one about
The Greatest Shepherd of All!" said Faith.

"I love that story! I'm so excited!" said Joy.

"I can't wait to hear it!" said Hope.

Grandpa Woolly grinned.
"Okay, come sit close to me and I'll tell you the story."

And with that, He began to tell
the most famous story in all sheepdom...

"One night there were three little sheep
out with their shepherds in a pasture.

In fact, they remind me
a lot of the three of you."

"Really? They were a lot like us? That's so neat!" exclaimed Joy.
"Shhh. I'm trying to listen," said Faith.
"I just want to hear the rest!" said Hope.

Grandpa Woolly cleared his throat and everyone got quiet again.
"The three little sheep were the most curious sheep
you could ever imagine. They got into all kinds of mischief."

Sawyer

Grandpa Woolly continued,
"When the shepherds carried these
three little sheep home after their adventures,
they often talked about a new Shepherd.

They said this new Shepherd was coming
to find all the lost sheep in the world.
The three little sheep thought
this new Shepherd sounded
pretty wonderful!

One night the three little sheep were eavesdropping
while the shepherds sat around the campfire.

Suddenly, the sky filled with light!

The sheep had never seen anything like it.
They darted behind the nearest bush.

Even their shepherds looked scared!

Sawyer

After their eyes adjusted to the bright light,
the sheep couldn't believe what they saw—an angel!

The angel said,

'Don't be afraid, I bring you
good news of great joy.'

Then the angel announced that
the new Shepherd had been born
in a town called Bethlehem.

When the angel finished telling the good news,
many more angels appeared and praised God!

Then the angels left and the sky was dark again.
But the shepherds were so happy they seemed to glow.

'He's here! He's here! Thank you, God!'
they shouted. 'Let's go find him!'

The three sheep knew what they wanted to do.
Go with the shepherds!

Very quietly, they began to sneak
through the darkness, following the shepherds.

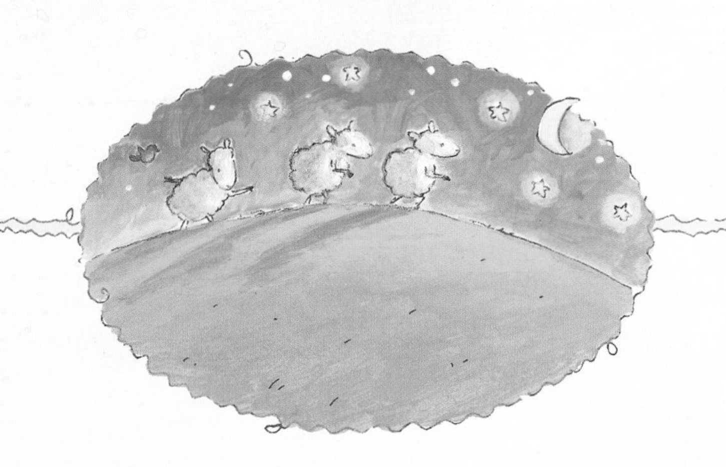

At first, following the shepherds seemed fun.
But after what felt like a long time of
walking through the darkness,
the three little sheep were getting tired.

'I've got to stop!' said one sheep.
The other two secretly wanted to rest too.
So they sat down on a patch of grass,
being sure to keep their eyes on the shepherds.
But they felt so tired that before they knew it,
they drifted off to sleep.

Z z z

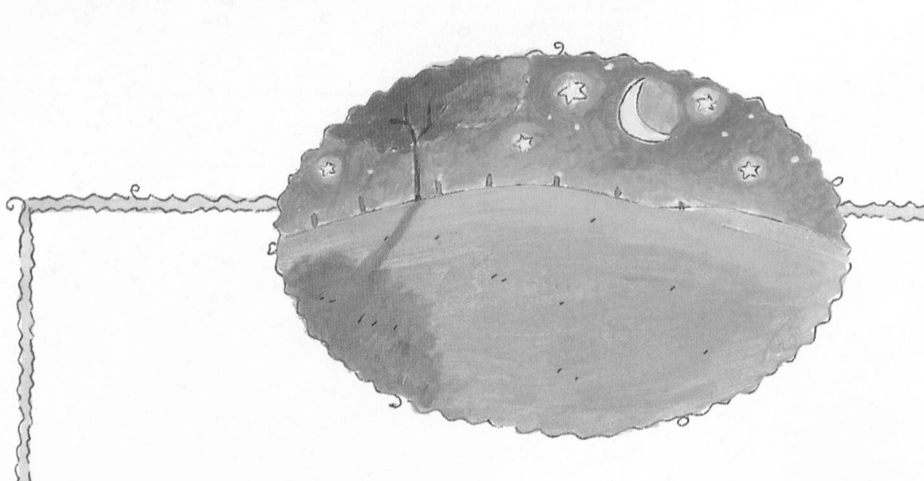

When they awoke, it was still dark
and the shepherds were nowhere in sight.

'what are we going to do?' exclaimed the first sheep.

'We have to go back,' said the second sheep.

'We can't go back! We've got to meet the new Shepherd,' said the third sheep.

They sat for a moment in silence.

The three little sheep thought about
the bright light, the angels,
and the new Shepherd who was coming
to find all the lost sheep.

Then deep down inside them,
a little voice seemed to whisper,
'Keep going.'

They knew what they had to do.
They got back on their hooves and looked around.

'Which way do you think they went?'
asked the first sheep.

'I don't know,'
said the second sheep with a sigh.

'I've been to Bethlehem before,'
said the third sheep.
'I think it's this way.'

They walked what seemed like a very long way.
Then they heard something
that every sheep fears.
An animal made a low noise behind them!

And it sounded like it was getting closer!
They ran as fast as they could.

Before they knew it,
they were at the edge of a steep hill.

The three little sheep looked back
at the large shadow moving toward them,
took a deep breath, and ran over the hill.

Soon they were tumbling,
tumbling,
tumbling down...
until they landed
in a cloud of dust at the bottom!"

Sawyer

Suddenly, the story was interrupted by little voices.

"Ooh, that sounds scary!" exclaimed Joy.

"I wouldn't have been scared," said Faith.

"Please tell us what happened next, Grandpa Woolly!"
whispered Hope.

Grandpa Woolly looked very serious.
Then he said, "They looked up and saw the animal
still standing at the top of the hill."

The little lambs gasped.

Then Grandpa Woolly said,
"But when they saw the animal,
they had to laugh at themselves.
It was just a silly cow!

The sheep looked at each other
and laughed some more.
They were covered in dirt!"

Faith, Hope, and Joy giggled and clapped.

"Hurray! I'm so glad they're okay!" exclaimed Joy.

"I knew they would be," said Faith.

"So did they meet the new Shepherd?" asked Hope.

Grandpa Woolly smiled and said,
"Well, let me finish the story and you'll find out."

Joy, Faith, and Hope got very quiet again
and Grandpa Woolly continued.

Sawyer

"The sun was just coming up and they could see a small village. A little girl was drawing water from a well. Maybe they could clean up there so the new Shepherd wouldn't see them like this! They hurried and scurried toward her.

'Look, Daddy! Sheep!' said the little girl, pointing at them. 'Good!' said her father. 'I'm going to market today and I could use a few more sheep.' The three little sheep gulped. If they were sold in the market, they would never get home again!

Before they could think of a way to escape, they were herded in with other sheep. The man began using a staff to make them walk down the road.

After what seemed like
many hours and miles,
the three little sheep finally arrived at the market.
Their hooves ached
and their hearts were heavy.
Now they would never meet the new Shepherd!

Just when the three little sheep
thought things were hopeless,
they saw something that made them jump for joy.

Their shepherds!

They began stomping their feet

and making as much noise

as they could.

Their shepherds turned and looked at them.

(Fortunately, they had kind and loving shepherds
who knew their sheep very well.)

'Hey, those are our sheep!' said one of the shepherds. 'How did they get here?' The shepherds talked to the man and before they knew it, the three little sheep were safe in their arms.

'You three get into more trouble than any sheep I've ever seen,' said one shepherd, but he was smiling. 'I know why you came,' said another. 'You wanted to meet the new Shepherd!' 'Well, now you'll get your chance,' said the third shepherd.

The sheep could hardly believe it. They really were going to meet the new Shepherd!

The shepherds carried them through the streets as evening set in. It was noisy, crowded, and dirty. The people seemed tired and confused, like they'd also had a very long day. They looked like they needed a shepherd too!

The shepherds brought them to an inn.
But instead of going inside,
they went to the stable just outside.

'Mary and Joseph,' one of the shepherds said,
'We've come back. And we've brought some of our sheep.
They were lost and we found them.
We hope you don't mind.'

Mary and Joseph smiled and let them in.
The shepherds set them down in front of the manger.
One of them said, 'Meet the new Shepherd!
His name is JESUS.'

The three little sheep
leaned over the edge
and peered inside.

This was the new Shepherd?
He was just a baby!

They looked inside again, closer this time.
The baby opened his eyes and looked at them.
The three sheep felt something in their hearts leap
when they looked into his face.

Suddenly, they didn't feel tired or dirty.
They felt peaceful and happy,
the happiest they had ever been!

And they felt clean—as white as snow.

Even if the rest of the world didn't realize it yet,

they knew this wasn't just any new shepherd.

This little baby was THE Shepherd.

The one God promised!

The shepherds let the sheep look at Baby Jesus

for a few moments. Then they said,

'Time to go home. We've got to share the good news!'

The three little sheep agreed.

This was the best news ever!

The shepherds praised God all the way home.
The three little sheep did too.

And from then on,
the sheep told everyone they met
about the new Shepherd
who was really

The Greatest Shepherd of All!"

Sawyer

Grandpa Woolly paused and then he said,
"So that's how three little sheep who were a lot like you met the Greatest Shepherd of All."

"That's why we celebrate Christmas, isn't it?" asked Faith.

"Yes," said Grandpa Woolly. "It absolutely is."

Faith nodded, "I knew it!"

“Do you think The Shepherd loves us?” asked Hope.

“Yes,” said Grandpa Woolly,
“He loves you very much.”

Grandpa Woolly noticed their eyes
were getting heavy
and he drew them closer around him.

Just before they drifted off to sleep,
Joy smiled and whispered,
"He really is a good Shepherd, isn't He?"

"Yes, Joy," said Grandpa Woolly,

"He really is
The Greatest Shepherd of All."